# KATIE WOO

## We Love You!

by Fran Manushkin

illustrated by Ta...

PICTURE WINDOW BOOKS
a capstone imprint

Katie Woo is published by Picture Window Books
a Capstone Imprint
1710 Roe Crest Drive
North Mankato, MN 56003
www.mycapstone.com

Text © 2018 Fran Manushkin
Illustrations © 2018 Picture Window Books

Cataloging-in-Publication Data is available on the
Library of Congress website.
ISBN: 978-1-5158-2277-6 (paperback)
ISBN: 978-1-5158-2279-0 (ebook)

Summary: From starting clubs to hosting sleepovers, Katie Woo is
one fun friend! Come along on her big adventures and funny mishaps.
Whether she's playing at home or working at school, everything
Katie does has us singing, "Katie Woo, we love you!"

Printed and bound in the USA.
082018  000043

# Table of Contents

# The Best
## Club

Katie was talking to JoJo. She said, "Wouldn't it be fun to be in a club?"

"For sure!" said JoJo. "It would be the best!"

Sophie Silver heard Katie
and JoJo.

"Guess what?" she said. "I'm
starting a club. It will be the best."

"Wow!" said Katie. "Can I be in your club?"

"I will think about it," said Sophie. "You have to be the best."

"Oh," said Katie.

She began to worry.

Yoko Moto asked Sophie, "Can I
be in your club? I'm a terrific artist."

"My paintings are better," said
Sophie. "I don't think you can be
in my club."

At recess, Fatima Ford said, "I can do three cartwheels. I am the best!"

"No way," said Sophie. "I can do four."

Fatima walked away, looking sad.

Katie told JoJo, "It's hard to be in Sophie's club. But I know what to do. Sophie loves pretty clothes. I will wear mine tomorrow."

The next day, Katie ran over to
Sophie, saying, "Don't I look great?
Now can I be in your club?"

"Sorry," said Sophie. "My dresses
are better."

Katie was sad all morning. She kept looking at Sophie and thinking. Katie thought very hard.

At recess, JoJo told Sophie,
"I don't think anyone can be the
best at everything."

"Well, I am!" shouted Sophie. "And you're not."

JoJo couldn't help it. She began to cry.

Katie looked at Sophie and said, "Sophie, you are right. You are the best."

Sophie smiled.

Katie added, "You are the best at being mean! That's what you are!"

Sophie stopped smiling.

"Katie is right," said Yoko Moto.
"Who would want to be in your club?"

"Nobody!" said JoJo. "Let's start our own club."

"That's the best idea," agreed Katie. "We will begin with a party! All the members can come."

"Yay!" yelled Fatima Ford and Yoko Moto.

They were so happy, they did four cartwheels.

Sophie walked away. She looked
sad. She looked sad all day.

After school, she got on the bus
looking sad.

Katie sat down next to Sophie.
She told her, "I know a secret."

Sophie looked at her. "What
secret?"

Katie whispered, "It's okay if
you are not the best."

"It is?" Sophie looked surprised.

"Yes." Katie smiled. "You just need to be yourself."

Sophie smiled back. "I can try that."

"It's easy," said JoJo. "I do it every day."

A few days later, Katie's club had their party.

They sang. They danced. They hugged. It was the best party ever!

# Katie's Spooky Sleepover

Katie was having a sleepover.

Mattie and JoJo came with their
pj's and their favorite dolls.

Janie, a new friend, said, "This is my first sleepover."

"Sleepovers are fun!" said Katie. "You'll see."

"First we eat," said Katie.

"Pizza is the best!" said Mattie.

"No!" yelled JoJo. "Cupcakes are!"

"Now let's play dress-up and make
fancy hats," said Katie.

"Yay, pom-poms!" said Mattie.

"Fuzzy feathers!" yelled JoJo.

"Shiny sparkles!" said Janie.

"Look at my fancy kimono,"
said Katie. "My dad got it in Japan.
He says it's lucky."

Everyone wanted to try it on.

Then they put on their pj's
and arranged their sleeping bags
in a circle.

"We all have flowers," said Janie.
"Katie's room looks like a garden."

Soon it was getting dark. "How about a ghost story?" said Mattie. "I love them."

"Great!" said Katie. She turned off the lights.

Mattie held a flashlight under her chin.

"Yikes!" yelled Janie. "Your face looks spooky!"

"My story is spooky too," said Mattie.

Mattie began. "Once upon a time, there was a monster. It had a big bony finger, and it went around the world poking people."

JoJo snuck up and poked Janie.

"Help!" she yelled. "It's the
monster!"

"It's me!" JoJo laughed.

"Now I'm worried," said Janie.
"Maybe there are monsters here."

"No way!" insisted Katie. "There are no monsters in my house!"

But that night, Katie had a spooky dream. She dreamed that a monster was under her bed!

Katie woke up early, still
thinking about her spooky dream.

"I'll put on my lucky kimono,"
she decided. "That will help me
feel better."

But her kimono was gone!

"Oh, no!" said Katie. "Maybe there is a monster under my bed. And he took my kimono."

Janie was still asleep, but Mattie
and JoJo were awake. Katie told
them about the monster.

"We have to look under your bed,"
said Mattie.

Mattie and Katie and JoJo were scared. But they held hands and looked under the bed.

"Yikes!" yelled Mattie. "Something poked me."

"It's the monster!" yelled Katie and JoJo.

"Surprise!" yelled Janie. "It's me."

"That was funny," said Katie.

"And you have my kimono!"

"I was scared," explained Janie,
"and I didn't have my teddy bear.
So I put on your lucky kimono. It
really helped."

"I'm glad," Katie said.

Then the girls got another
surprise.

"Guess what's for breakfast?"
said Katie's mom. "Ghost pancakes."

"Wow!" joked JoJo. "More
spooks!"

Janie said, "This is the best sleepover!"

"For sure!" agreed Mattie and JoJo.

"Now," said Katie, "let's make the last ghost disappear."

And they shared the last pancake.

# Katie Blows
# Her Top

Katie was feeling tip-top.

She told her dad, "Today I'm going to learn about volcanoes. It will be a blast!"

On the way to school, Pedro said, "Volcanoes are awesome! But I don't want to be near one."

"I do," said Katie. "I want to hear the KABOOM!"

Miss Winkle told the class, "When hot melted rock and gas reach the top of the mountain, BOOM! The volcano explodes. It can bury a city!"

"Sometimes we know when a volcano blast is coming," said Miss Winkle. "Sometimes it's a surprise."

"I have a surprise for you," said Miss Winkle. "Today, we are making volcanoes! We will work in teams."

Katie picked JoJo and Pedro.

Miss Winkle gave them some clay and a bottle.

She said, "The first step is to mold this clay around the bottle. Try to make the shape of a mountain."

Pedro grabbed all the clay and tried to make a mountain.

"Stop!" said Katie. "Our mountain
is lumpy!"

"Lumpy is fun," Pedro said.

"No!" said Katie. "Lumpy
is wrong!"

"The clay will need time to dry,"
said Miss Winkle. "We will finish
our volcanoes after lunch."

During lunch, Katie told
Pedro, "Don't be a volcano hog.
I want to do the rest! I know I
can make it explode."

"Hey!" yelled JoJo. "What
about me?"

After lunch, Miss Winkle gave
each team white vinegar and red
food coloring to mix in a bowl.

"Let's make the lava super red," said Katie.

Oops! She poured in too much, and the red spilled on her shirt.

"Yuck!" Katie groaned. "What a mess!"

"The next step," said Miss Winkle, "is to pour baking soda on a paper towel."

"I'll do it," said Pedro.

"No. Me!" said JoJo.

JoJo tried to grab the baking
soda. Oops! The baking soda went
flying and landed on Katie's head!

"Yikes!" yelled JoJo. "You are
a mess!"

KABOOM!

That's when Katie blew her top. Her cheeks got hot and red, and she made angry faces.

Boy, did Katie make faces!

"Wow!" said Pedro. "You are fierce! You said you wanted to be close to a volcano. And you are! You became a volcano!"

"I am a volcano?" said Katie.
"Wowzee! Sometimes I *am* a little
fierce."

"For sure," agreed Miss Winkle.
She sent Katie to clean up.

Later, JoJo told Katie, "Let's start a new volcano, and this time we will be fair. We will each do our share."

Katie did the last step: She poured the baking soda into the bottle.

When it mixed with the vinegar —

KABOOM!

The lava poured out. "Wow!"
shouted everyone. "Awesome!"

"High five!" said Katie and Pedro
and JoJo.

After school, Katie said, "Let's be volcanoes all the way home."

Boy, did they yell!

"Kaboom!"

"Kaboom!"

"KABOOOOOM!"

Daddy Can't
Dance

You are cordially invited to the

Daddy-Daughter Dance

Friday   6:00 pm

Dinner, dessert, and dancing.

"Look at this letter," said Katie's
dad. "We are invited to a dance."

"Cool!" said Katie. "Is it a ballet?
I love to watch ballet."

"It's a daddy-daughter dance," said her father. "*We* will be dancing."

"Cool!" said Katie, twirling around. "I'm a good dancer."

"I'm a good dancer too," said
Katie's dad. "I'm good at stepping
on your mom's toes."

"For sure!" said Katie's mom.

"Don't worry," Katie told her dad. "We have lots of time. I can teach you."

"Great," said her dad. "I want you to be proud of me."

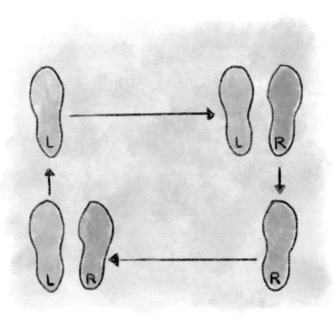

"Let's start with a slow dance,"
said Katie. "See how I am dancing
in a square?"

"I see," said her dad.

Katie's dad put his arms around
Katie. He smiled and said, "So far,
so good."

Then they began dancing.

After two steps, Katie yelled,

"Ouch! You stepped on my foot."

"Sorry!" said her dad.

"Let's try again," said Katie.

Oops! She tripped over her dad's foot.

"Your feet are big," said Katie. "Dancing with you is tricky."

"I can do a fast dance," said her father. "See? Nobody's toes get in the way."

Katie's mom danced too. She was awesome.

The next day, Pedro came over.

He was a terrific dancer.

"I love to kick when I dance,"
he said. "It's like playing soccer."

"You can't kick in a slow dance," said Katie. "I will be wearing a fancy dress, and a slow dance is dreamy."

A few days later, JoJo and Katie went shopping for fancy dresses.

"The blue dress is pretty," said Katie. "But this red dress is dreamier. I pick red."

But on the day of the dance,
Katie told her dad, "Maybe I should
have picked the blue dress."

"No way," said her dad. "Red is a
lucky color. I even got a tie to match it."

At the gym, Katie and her dad
said hi to Yoko and her uncle and
Mattie and her grandpa.

"Cool dress," said Mattie.

Katie smiled and said, "Red
is the color of luck."

The first dance was a fast one.

"I can do that," said Katie's dad.

He was terrific.

JoJo and her dad waved at them.

The gym was rocking!

Then a slow dance started.
Katie's dad looked worried. He said,
"Let's rest now."

So they sat down and watched
the dreamy dancers.

"My new shoes feel tight," said Katie. She took them off to wiggle her toes.

Katie looked at her bare feet and her dad's big, hard shoes. "Ha!" she said. "I have an idea."

"This is how we can do a slow dance," said Katie. "I'll dance on your feet!"

"Wow!" He smiled. "I can *do* this."

They danced and danced.

Katie's dad felt proud. So
did Katie.

"What a cool idea," said Katie's
friends. They danced on toes too.

When they got home, Katie and her dad showed her mom their dance.

"Lovely!" said Katie's mom.

Before bedtime, Katie hugged her dress and did a few last spins.

She felt very lucky!

# Having Fun with Katie Woo!

## Peanut Butter and Jelly Sushi

Club meetings are even more fun when members can share a snack. Here is a tasty, easy recipe. You could even make it a club activity and prepare it together. Make sure to ask a grown-up for permission and help if you need it!

### Ingredients:

- 1 loaf of sliced bread
- peanut butter
- jelly (flavor of your choice)

### Other things you need:

- sharp knife
- rolling pin
- butter knife
- cutting board

**What you do:**

1. Cut the crusts from a slice of bread using the sharp knife.

2. With the rolling pin, flatten each strip of bread.

3. Use the butter knife to spread a layer of peanut butter on the bread. Repeat with jelly.

4. Starting at one end, roll up the bread. Repeat steps 1 through 4 with the rest of the bread.

5. Using the sharp knife, slice each roll into 1-inch pieces on the cutting board.

To make your treat extra special, serve the rolls on a pretty platter and try eating them with chopsticks!

# Fabulous Flowers

Men sometimes wear small flowers on their jackets on special occasions. They are called boutonnieres (pronounced boo-tuhn-EERS). You can make your own boutonniere out of tissue paper and give it to your special guy!

## What you need:

- colorful tissue paper
- scissors
- green pipe cleaners
- marker
- small cup

## What you do:

1. Layer the tissue paper until you have 8 to 12 layers together.

2. Lay the cup on the paper. Using the marker, trace the cup to make a circle.

3. Cut out the circle, cutting through all the layers of tissue paper.

4. Using the tip of the scissors make two small circles, about an inch apart, in the center of the circle.

5. Insert a pipe cleaner through one hole. Then loop it down into the second hole. Twist the pipe cleaner around itself so it is secure. This is your stem.

6. Layer by layer, scrunch the paper up, scrunching it in slightly different directions with each layer. This is your flower!

7. If needed, trim the pipe cleaner so it is about 4 inches long. You can also shape a leaf out of another piece of pipe cleaner and twist it around the stem to secure.

# About the Author

Fran Manushkin is the author of many popular picture books, including *Happy in Our Skin*; *Baby, Come Out!*; *Latkes and Applesauce: A Hanukkah Story*; *The Tushy Book*; *Big Girl Panties*; *Big Boy Underpants*; and *Bamboo for Me, Bamboo for You*. There is a real Katie Woo — she's Fran's great-niece — but she never gets in half the trouble of the Katie Woo in the books. Fran writes on her beloved Mac computer in New York City, without the help of her two naughty cats, Chaim and Goldy.

# About the Illustrator

Tammie Lyon began her love for drawing at a young age while sitting at the kitchen table with her dad. She continued her love of art and eventually attended the Columbus College of Art and Design, where she earned a bachelor's degree in fine art. After a brief career as a professional ballet dancer, she decided to devote herself full time to illustration. Today she lives with her husband, Lee, in Cincinnati, Ohio. Her dogs, Gus and Dudley, keep her company as she works in her studio.